★ NEW Adventures

MY NEW
FRIEND

Franklin Watts

First published in Great Britain in 2018
by The Watts Publishing Group
Copyright © The Watts Publishing Group 2018
All rights reserved

Managing editor: Victoria Brooker
Creative design: Paul Cherrill

ISBN: 978 1 445 1 5902 7 (hbk)
ISBN: 978 1 445 1 5903 4 (pbk)

Printed in China

Franklin Watts
An imprint of Hachette Children's Group
Part of The Watts Publishing Group
Carmelite House
50 Victoria Embankment
London EC4Y 0DZ
An Hachette UK Company

www.hachette.co.uk
www.franklinwatts.co.uk

My NEW FRIEND

Written by
TOM EASTON

Illustrated by
CHARLIE ALDER

FRANKLIN WATTS
LONDON • SYDNEY

I'm sad. Mum told me today that my best friend Sophie is moving to another country! Sophie lives on my street and we spend ALL our time together.

We play in the park
down the road,

we go to swimming
lessons together,

and we walk to school
together every day.

We play Cat's Cradle for ages every day too and are getting really good at it. We were going to be World Champions at Cat's Cradle but now that will never happen. It's just not fair.

On the day Sophie left, I cried for ages.
Mum and my cat, Colin, tried to cheer me up.
"You'll make new friends soon," Mum said.
"I don't want new friends," I replied. "I just want Sophie."

The next day, we walked to school alone. It was raining.
Mum kept trying to be all cheerful and she told me we could
get an ice cream on the way home.
It's too cold and wet for ice cream, I thought,
but I said thank you anyway and tried to cheer up.

When I walked into the classroom, there was an empty
seat next to me and I got sad all over again.
"At least I get a double desk to myself," I thought.

"Now, children," Miss Shah said, "we have a new pupil starting with us today. "Her name is Emily. I'd like you all to make her feel welcome." I looked up to see a new girl standing next to Miss Shah. She looked nervous.

"There's an empty seat next to Ginny," Miss Shah said, pointing in my direction. That's Sophie's seat, I thought as Emily came to sit next to me.

I couldn't really concentrate on the lesson and when Miss Shah asked me a question I didn't know what the answer was. "Come on, Ginny," Miss Shah said. "You can do this."

I felt like bursting into tears,
but then Emily whispered "four".
"Four!" I called and Miss Shah nodded.
"Very good," she said and turned
back to the whiteboard.
"Thanks," I whispered.
"You're welcome," Emily said, and we
smiled at each other.

At break-time, we all rushed outside. I saw Emily sit on her own
on the buddy bench. That's where you go if you have no-one
to play with. I just wanted to be on my own because I was so sad.
But then I thought about how lonely and nervous Sophie
must be on the first day in her new school.

I hoped someone would go and be her friend. It was just the same with Emily and I wondered if she'd left her best friend behind too. I walked up to her.

"Would you like to play Cat's Cradle?" I asked.
"I don't know how," Emily replied. "But I really like skipping."
So Emily taught me a skipping routine.

Then I tried to
teach her Cat's Cradle.
We both kept getting
it wrong and couldn't
stop laughing.

After school, I ran up to Mum and dragged
her over to meet Emily and her mum.
"Can Emily come to our house for a play date at the weekend?" I asked.
"Of course," Mum replied, laughing. "If that's OK with Emily's mum?"

"Definitely," Emily's mum said. "I'm pleased
she's made a new friend already."
I was very excited about the play date.
We'd go to the park and play Cat's Cradle
then maybe have an ice cream!

But the next day, when
I got to school, I saw Emily playing
with some other girls.

They were skipping and they
were really good at it.

The other girls weren't really my friends. I sat on
my own under the tree and watched for a while. I got sad
all over again because Emily is MY new friend.
"I don't want to lose another friend,"
I said to myself. I miss Sophie.

"Hi Ginny," someone said.
"Come and join our game."
I looked up. It was Emily.

"I'm not very good at skipping,"
I said. "Not like those other girls."
"Don't worry," she said. "You just
need some more practice."
"And I don't really know those girls,"
I said. "They're not even in our class."
"They're nice," Emily said. "I'll introduce you."

Emily introduced me to the other girls. Their names were Aisha and Imogen. They showed me how to do a very simple skipping routine. And guess what? I learned how to do it really quickly. Maybe I could be World Champion at skipping instead of Cat's Cradle.

Then I tripped over and fell and everyone was worried that
I'd hurt myself but I bounced back up and carried on with the skipping.
"Well done, Ginny!" Emily cried. When the bell rang, Emily grabbed
my hand and we went into the classroom together.

On Saturday, Emily came over. It was raining so we couldn't go to
the park and get an ice cream. I showed her some more moves
in Cat's Cradle. We played for a while, but then Emily said.
"Can we play something else now?"
"Like what?" I said. "How about a board game?"

I was a bit cross at first.
We'd never win the World
Championship unless
we practised loads.
But I got out a board
game and I had to admit
we had lots of fun.
I laughed until my
stomach hurt.

When Emily's mum came around to pick her up,
I didn't want her to go. I gave her a big hug
and even Colin came over for a last stroke.

"I think Colin likes Emily," Mum said once they'd gone.
"I like her too," I said. "She's my new best friend!"

Notes for Parents and Teachers

Making new friends can be difficult for children, especially if they are naturally shy, or find themselves in a new situation, such as moving to a new school, or if a best friend suddenly moves away. Helping your child to make new friends can be challenging and may take time. Encourage your child to get to know as many classmates as possible and to talk to you about them if they want to. Ask your child what they like about each of their classmates.

Show your child how to be friendly. Encourage them to smile and be kind. Remember, children learn best when they observe the right behaviour at home too, so make a point of showing warmth and kindness to your own friends.

Try enrolling your child in a new music, sport or creative class to broaden their social horizons. It is natural for children to be drawn to the most popular, outgoing or athletic children in their class, but friendships are about sharing interests. Whilst it might not be helpful to be too prescriptive about who your child chooses to be friends with, you may be able to help out by inviting children for a playdate if you feel they might share similar interests and characteristics with your child.

Encourage a variety of friends. Your child could have a football friend, a LEGO-making friend and a walking-to-school friend. Explain that there's no reason they need to choose between them. And make sure they understand the importance of being kind to friends of friends. The more the merrier!

Children are often very good at working out solutions for themselves, so try and get them to come up with some ideas that will help them to feel less anxious about finding a new friend. You can certainly help with some suggestions but allow them to be in charge as to what will work best for them. Suggest your child performs an act of kindness to their new friend. Baking them cupcakes, or inviting them to come along on a family day out.

As a parent it is natural to worry but try not to show this anxiety to your child. Be positive, patient and understanding.

Websites for Parents

www.netmums.com

www.helpiammoving.com/moving_house/moving_with_children.php

www.thespruce.com/help-kids-settle-into-new-school-2436191

www.gettherightschool.co.uk/should-you-move-your-child-different-school.html

www.theschoolrun.com/settling-into-a-new-school

www.gov.uk/government/publications/moving-school-packs

Books To Share

My New Friend
by Jillian Powell, Wayland, 2011

Be a Friend
by Salina Yoon, Bloomsbury, 2016

Pip and Posy: The New Friend
by Axel Scheffler, Nosy Crow Ltd, 2017

Topsy and Tim: Make a New Friend
by Jean and Gareth Adamson, Ladybird, 2003

Ebb and Flo and Their New Friend
by Jane Simmons, Orchard, 2005

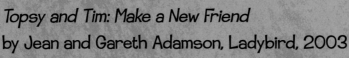